W9-ACD-382

Will You Give Me a Dream?

Joan Lowery Nixon

ILLUSTRATED BY Bruce Degen

FOUR WINDS PRESS ✳ New York

MAXWELL MACMILLAN CANADA Toronto
MAXWELL MACMILLAN INTERNATIONAL
New York Oxford Singapore Sydney

Four Winds Press
Macmillan Publishing Company
866 Third Avenue
New York, NY 10022
Maxwell Macmillan Canada, Inc.
1200 Eglinton Avenue East
Suite 200
Don Mills, Ontario M3C 3N1
Macmillan Publishing Company is part of the
Maxwell Communication Group of Companies.
First edition
Printed and bound in the United States of America

10 9 8 7 6 5 4 3 2 1

The text of this book is set in Goudy Old Style.
The illustrations are rendered in pencil, watercolor and gouache.
Book design by Christy Hale

Library of Congress Cataloging-in-Publication Data
Nixon, Joan Lowery.
Will you give me a dream? / Joan Lowery Nixon ; illustrated by Bruce Degen.
    p.   cm.
Summary: Matthew's mother gives him the beginnings of a dream to help him go to sleep.
ISBN 0-02-768211-0
[1. Dreams—Fiction. 2. Bedtime—Fiction.] I. Degen, Bruce,
ill. II. Title.
PZ7.N65Wi 1994
[E]—dc20   91-19581

With love to my grandson,
Matthew Joseph Nixon
—J.L.N.

For Chris, Kim, Christopher
and Matthew Schmitt
—Thanks
and for Emma and Marcus Fischer
—Bow Wow
—B.D.

Matthew had tried to sleep. He had even squeezed his eyes tightly shut. But he couldn't sleep.

So Matthew pushed his bathtub boat through the waves he'd
made with his covers. He growled loud thunder noises and
bounced on the bed.

Matthew still didn't feel sleepy. He leaned over the bed to where fat, furry Buster lay curled on the rug, snorting and snuffling in his deep dog dreams. Matthew rolled his boat across Buster's back with a *swish-swish-swish*, but Buster slept on.

Matthew heard the door to his bedroom open. He looked up at Mother and said, "I can't sleep."

"Of course you can't," Mother said. "It's hard to fall asleep while you're doing somersaults in your bed."

She stepped over Buster and straightened the top sheet and quilt on Matthew's bed, tucking them under his chin as she gave him a kiss.

"You had your story and your drink of water," she said. "Now it's time to settle down and go to sleep."

"I *can't* sleep," Matthew said. "I don't have a dream." He squirmed out from under the covers and held up his arms to his mother. "Will you let me sit on your lap? Will you give me a dream?"

Mother picked him up, sat in the rocking chair, and held him close. She took the boat from his hand and put it on the toy chest. "Snuggle up, Matthew, and I'll give you a dream," she said. "How would you like it to begin?"

Matthew thought a moment. "Last time I rode into my dream on a big black horse," he said. "This time I want to fly."

"Then I'll give you a sea gull with wings that spread wider than your arms can reach," Mother told him. "His silver feathers gleam in the moonlight and sparkle back at the stars.

"Hop on his back. It's as soft as your pillow and cradles you as he soars into the purple sky."

"He's my sea gull, and nobody else's," Matthew said. "A long, long time ago I found him. I fed him bugs and cookies and hamburgers, and now we're friends."

"Up in the air you go," Mother said. "Do you feel the brush of cool wind against your cheek? And the tickle-smell of ocean salt in your nose?"

Matthew shivered and snuggled closer.

"Your sea gull dives," Mother told him. "Hold tightly! He skims just over the water, and you see the dark shapes of fish dart and swarm beneath the rippled surface.

"Then up he goes again. Higher you fly. Higher. You look down, and what do you see?"

"Something," Matthew said. "I know. It's a boat. A boat with a white sail."

"A sailing ship," Mother said. "You can see the blinking
lights. I wonder who is on the ship."

"I'll find out," Matthew said. "My sea gull will take me
there. He knows where I want to go."

"Tell me what you see," Mother said. "There must be a captain and crew."

"Yes," Matthew said, "but they aren't people. They're dogs....Big dogs and little dogs, fuzzy dogs, and fat dogs like Buster."

"What does the captain look like?" Mother asked.

"He's a great big gray dog, as big as me," Matthew said. "And he's wearing a sailor suit and a crown."

"A crown? That's strange," Mother said.

"No, it isn't strange," Matthew explained. "A captain can wear anything he likes."

"You're right," Mother said.

She frowned. "Oh, dear. All the dogs are crying. The captain is howling. Big tears roll down his face and plop onto the deck. Something must be wrong with the ship. Can you see what it is?"

"Yes! I see what's wrong!" Matthew told Mother. "The ship is broken. The part that holds the sail is broken, and the sail is in the water."

Mother sighed and asked, "What will those poor dogs do? They can't repair their ship. They aren't strong enough to mend the mast and pull the sail from the water. They need someone strong to help them."

"I'll help them," Matthew said. He bent an arm and flexed his muscles. "I'm strong enough."

"Of course you're strong enough," Mother said, "and think how happy the dogs will be when you rescue them. I'm sure that the captain will let you wear his gold crown and invite you to steer the ship and take his crew across the deep water."

Matthew thought about it. "Where will I take them?" he asked.

"Your dream can go wherever you like," Mother said. "You have the stars to light your way, your sea gull to guide you, and this hug and kiss to take with you."

As Matthew climbed off Mother's lap, Buster gave a gentle
snore. Mother tucked Matthew into bed, and he shut his eyes.
The sound of the waves splashing against the sides of the ship
was so loud he could barely hear the closing of his bedroom
door.

With a little help from the crew, Matthew fastened the mast
into place. As the sails billowed out in the wind and the ship
began to move, the dogs laughed and cheered. Some of them
threw colored streamers.

The captain was happy to let Matthew wear his crown and steer the ship. He settled comfortably into a deck chair with a cup of hot cocoa. "Where are we going?" he asked.

The sea gull swooped toward the south, and Matthew spun the wheel to follow. "To magical places," Matthew told the captain. "Wait and see."